For Michael,
who gave me the title
and who is always on time
—A. A.

For the Kellaway sisters—Michelle, Sara, and Natasha
—S.M-N.

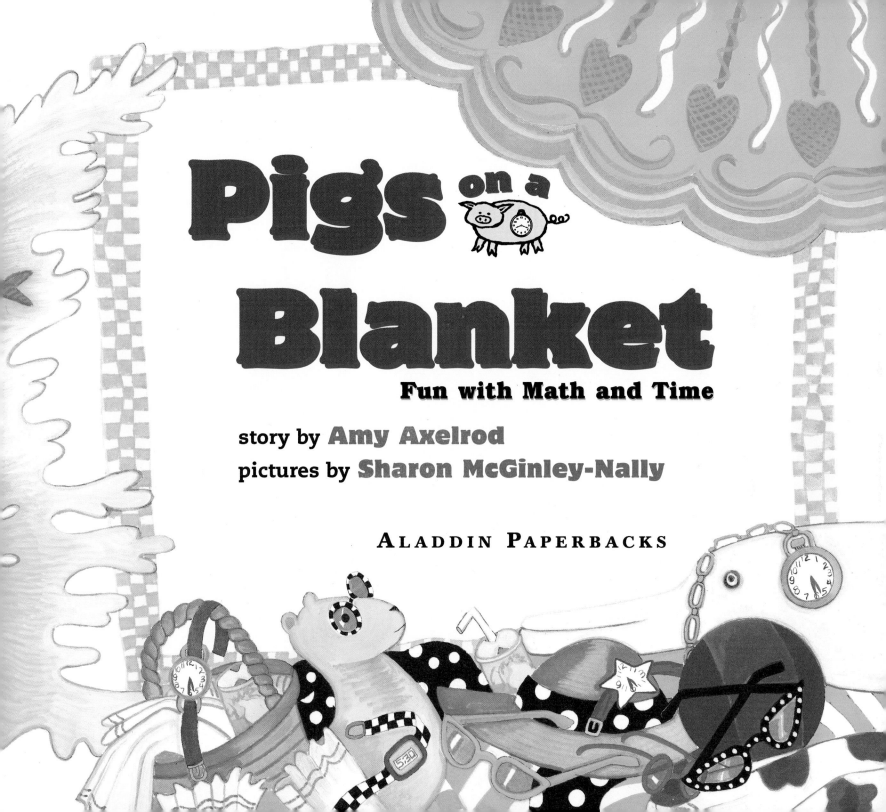

Pigs on a Blanket

Fun with Math and Time

story by **Amy Axelrod**

pictures by **Sharon McGinley-Nally**

ALADDIN PAPERBACKS

The Pigs were in a rut.

"We need a change of pace," said Mrs. Pig. "We've been glued to this couch for hours."

"Let's spend the day at the beach," suggested Mr. Pig.

"Great idea," said Mrs. Pig, "except for one thing."

"What's that?" asked Mr. Pig.

"The beach is an hour's drive from here," she said. "Don't you think we'd be getting a late start?"

Mr. Pig looked at his watch. It was 11:30. "No problem," he said. "We can be on the road in no time."

"Well then, family," said Mrs. Pig.

READY, SET, GO!

In just ten minutes, the piglets changed into
swimsuits, packed beach toys, and blew up their floats.

Five minutes later, Mrs. Pig came downstairs wearing
a new swimsuit and toting a bag filled with towels,
hats, a blanket, sun lotion, and her favorite book.
They waited . . . and waited . . . and waited
for Mr. Pig.

"It's about time!" scolded
Mrs. Pig. "We've been sitting
here for a good forty-five minutes.
At this rate, we'll never ride the waves."
"Sorry, dear," said Mr. Pig. "I had a tough
time finding a swimsuit that fit. I guess I've
put on a few pounds since last year."
"Never mind," said Mrs. Pig. "Let's hurry now."

At 12:45, the Pigs were in the car and all set to leave
for the beach when Mr. Pig discovered that he didn't
have the car keys.

"They must be here somewhere," said Mrs. Pig.

"What do you know!" said Mr. Pig one hour later
as he bent over to look under the car. "The keys were in
my pocket all along."

Finally the Pigs were on the road.
Mr. Pig made good time for
three quarters of an hour.

But then he reached a railroad crossing. Twenty-five
minutes later the caboose passed, and the Pigs were
once again on their way.

"Almost at the beach," said Mrs. Pig. "I can smell it
in the air."

"We need a bathroom," said the piglets.
"It's an emergency."

"But we just passed a rest area right before the train crossing," said Mr. Pig. "Can't you wait? We'll be at the beach in just ten minutes. There's a bathroom there."

The piglets shook their heads no. "Hurry," they said.

Mr. Pig beat the clock. He made a U-turn and reached the rest area in only two minutes. While the piglets visited the bathrooms, Mr. Pig visited with a police officer who wrote him a speeding ticket. Thirteen minutes later, the police officer sent the Pigs on their way.

At 3:30, the Pigs arrived at the beach.
"We're hungry," said the piglets.

Mrs. Pig and the piglets made
themselves comfortable on the blanket
while Mr. Pig went to the snack bar.

"I wonder what is keeping your
father," said Mrs. Pig to the piglets.
"He's been gone a long time."

BEACH
CLOSES
5:30

A total of sixty minutes passed before Mr. Pig returned.

"The line was very long," he explained, "but it was worth the wait. Look what I brought for us to eat . . . triple-decker cheese sandwiches, chips, lemonade, and brownies."

The Pigs ate their food in ten minutes.

"We're roasting," said the piglets. "Can we go swimming now?"

"In due time," said Mrs. Pig. "Let's see, we each had a triple-decker cheese sandwich. That alone is a twenty-minute wait. Then figure ten more minutes for the chips."

"Dear, don't forget the lemonade and those delicious brownies," said Mr. Pig.

Mrs. Pig thought for a second. "Mmmm, you're right. I'm adding on an extra twenty minutes," she said, "just to be on the safe side."

The Pigs decided to pass the time relaxing on the blanket.

When their stomachs settled, Mrs. Pig said,
"Okay, family, it's time to ride the waves!"

Mr. Pig led the charge to the water. "Your mother's right, kids,"
he said. "It's time to ride the . . ."

How Did the Pigs Run Out of Time?

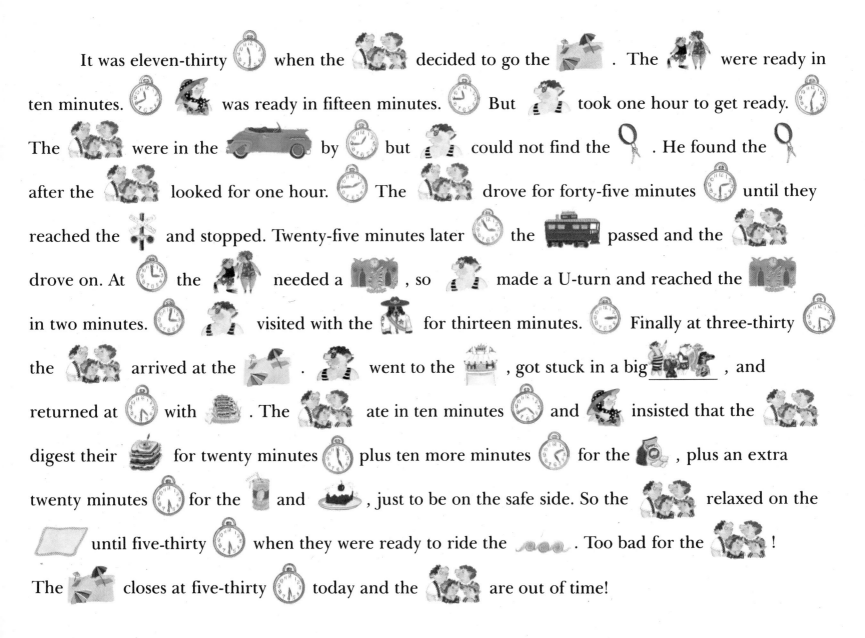

It was eleven-thirty when the decided to go the . The were ready in ten minutes. was ready in fifteen minutes. But took one hour to get ready. The were in the by but could not find the . He found the after the looked for one hour. The drove for forty-five minutes until they reached the and stopped. Twenty-five minutes later the passed and the drove on. At the needed a , so made a U-turn and reached the in two minutes. visited with the for thirteen minutes. Finally at three-thirty the arrived at the . went to the , got stuck in a big _____ , and returned at with . The ate in ten minutes and insisted that the digest their for twenty minutes plus ten more minutes for the , plus an extra twenty minutes for the and , just to be on the safe side. So the relaxed on the until five-thirty when they were ready to ride the . Too bad for the ! The closes at five-thirty today and the are out of time!

First Aladdin Paperbacks edition August 1998
Text copyright © 1996 by Amy Axelrod. Illustrations copyright © 1996 by Sharon McGinley-Nally

Aladdin Paperbacks
An imprint of Simon & Schuster Children's Publishing Division
1230 Avenue of the Americas, New York, NY 10020

Designed by Anahid Hamparian
The text of this book is set in 17-point Baskerville. The illustrations are rendered in inks, watercolors and acrylics.

Printed and bound in the United States of America   10 9 8 7 6 5 4 3 2 1
The Library of Congress has cataloged the hardcover edition as follows:
Axelrod, Amy. Pigs on a blanket / by Amy Axelrod; pictures by Sharon McGinley-Nally.
p.   cm.   Summary: Because the Pig family has so many delays in getting to the beach,
when they finally are ready to swim they find that the beach is closed.
ISBN 0-689-80505-5   [1. Pigs–Fiction. 2. Beaches–Fiction. 3. Time–Fiction.] I. McGinley-Nally, Sharon, ill. II. Title.
PZ7.A96155Ph 1996 [E]–dc20 95-3677
ISBN 0-689-82252-9 (Aladdin pbk.)

Time Facts

60 seconds=1 minute
60 minutes=1 hour
24 hours=1 day

The long hand of a clock is called the minute hand. It
goes around the clock once every hour. The short hand of a clock
is called the hour hand. It goes around the clock twice every day, once for the A.M. hours
(between midnight and noon) and once for the P.M. hours (between noon and midnight).

Some clocks have a very small hand, called the second hand. It goes around the clock
once every minute. Some clocks do not have a face or hands. They are called digital
clocks. The numbers, or digits, on the clock are displayed just as they would be written.
For example: 3:00·10 is the same as

How long does it actually take the Pigs to drive to the beach?
How much longer is the drive than it should have been?
Bonus question: *How long does Mrs. Pig decide that the Pigs have to wait before they can*
ride the waves?

Dear Pig Fans,

Pigs On A Blanket: Fun With Math and Time is the second title in the Pigs Will Be Pigs math series. It's all about MEASURING TIME! When I was in elementary school, those words frightened me, as did just about everything that had to do with math. I never realized that math was all around us in our daily lives. That's why I wrote the Pigs Will Be Pigs books, which (by the way) are all based on true family adventures. We love to go to the beach, but if we don't leave the house early enough, we get caught in heavy traffic. One time, we left *so* early that the parking lot attendant wasn't even there when we arrived at the beach! That's when I had a great idea—having the Pigs waste time getting to the beach would be a fun way to learn about measuring intervals of time. So follow these easy steps:

1) Read **Pigs On A Blanket** just for fun!

2) Go back and read the story again. Match the pictures to the words. Whenever a time is mentioned in the story, it is shown on the Pigs' watches in the illustrations.

3) Practice telling time. Time yourself doing things. How long does it take you to eat breakfast? To brush your teeth? To read **Pigs On A Blanket?**

4) Answer the math questions at the end of the book. You can do this by yourself, with your parents, or with your teacher.

Remember the Pig Family Motto:

MATH + READING = FUN

Love,
Amy Axelrod

P.S. For Parents and Teachers Only
The Pigs Will Be Pigs books have been designed around the National Council of Teachers of Mathematics's Thirteen Standards. Use them as picture book read-alouds initially, and then as vehicles to introduce, reinforce, and review the concepts and skills particular to each title.